AMAZON BOY

WRITTEN AND ILLUSTRATED BY TED LEWIN

Macmillan Publishing Company   New York
Maxwell Macmillan Canada   Toronto
Maxwell Macmillan International   New York   Oxford   Singapore   Sydney

In memory of Chico Mendes

SOME TERMS USED IN THIS BOOK:

Açai—fruit of the palm tree
Manioc—also called cassava,
   it is grown for its edible root.
Tucupi—manioc sauce.

Library of Congress Cataloging-in-Publication Data. Lewin, Ted. Amazon boy / written and illustrated by Ted Lewin. — 1st ed. p.   cm. Summary: As a Brazilian boy makes his first trip up the Amazon to the port city of Belém, he learns something about the river's many treasures. ISBN 0-02-757383-4. [1. Brazil—Fiction. 2. Amazon River Region—Fiction. 3. Environmental protection—Fiction.] I. Title. PZ7.L58419Am 1993   [E]—dc20   92-15798

Paulo was so excited he couldn't fish. Tomorrow was his birthday, and he and his father were going to Belém, the great city near the mouth of the Amazon River.

Paulo and his family lived deep in
the Amazon jungle where they fished
and planted manioc. In all his young
life, Paulo had never been downriver.

Long before he saw the old steamer chugging around the
bend, Paulo heard its whistle blow. He ran to the riverbank
and waited.

"We will go to the old part of the city, the harbor, and the market," said Paulo's father as the boat swung into midriver. "I want you to see the gifts our great river gives us."

They passed small settlements at the edge of the rain forest, and many boats along the way.

Early the next morning Paulo's father gently shook him awake. "Paulo, come and see!" There it was, the harbor guarded by its old stone fort, and a huge cast-iron building with four pointed turrets. The tide was out and the fishing boats with their colorful sails were lying in the mud, bellies exposed.

They left the steamer and joined the early morning crowds. Paulo had never seen so many people. The fishermen were selling fish on the dock, or cooking breakfast in pots on the slanting decks of their boats.

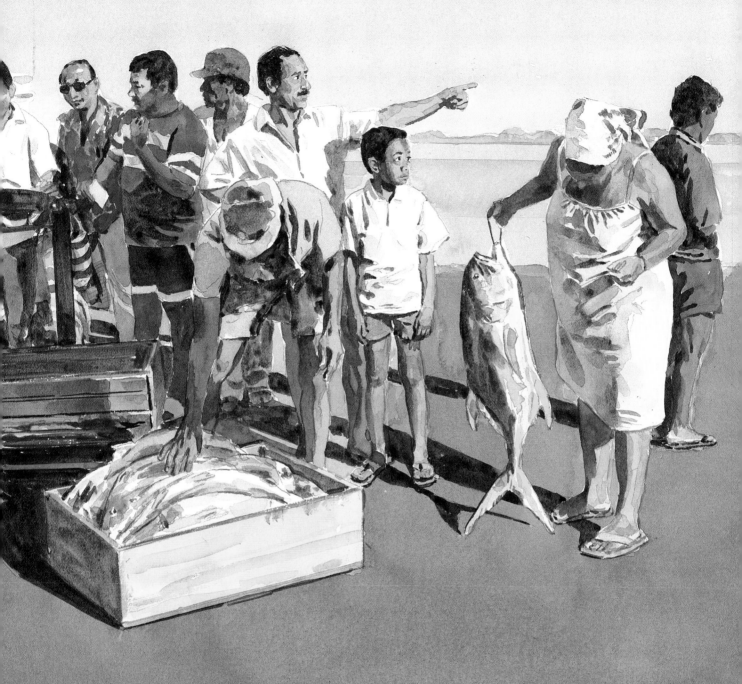

There were red fish, golden fish, and silver fish. Fish that looked like toads. Fish that looked like snakes. So many different kinds of fish. "Some come from the ocean, out there," said Paulo's father, "and some come from the Amazon."

There were men carrying boxes full of fish on their heads. A short, thick-necked man pushed through the crowd carrying a huge fish.

"That's a *filhote*," said Paulo's father. "They used to be twice that size, but all the really big ones have been caught. No one ever thought of the future. Now they are smaller. Someday there will be none."

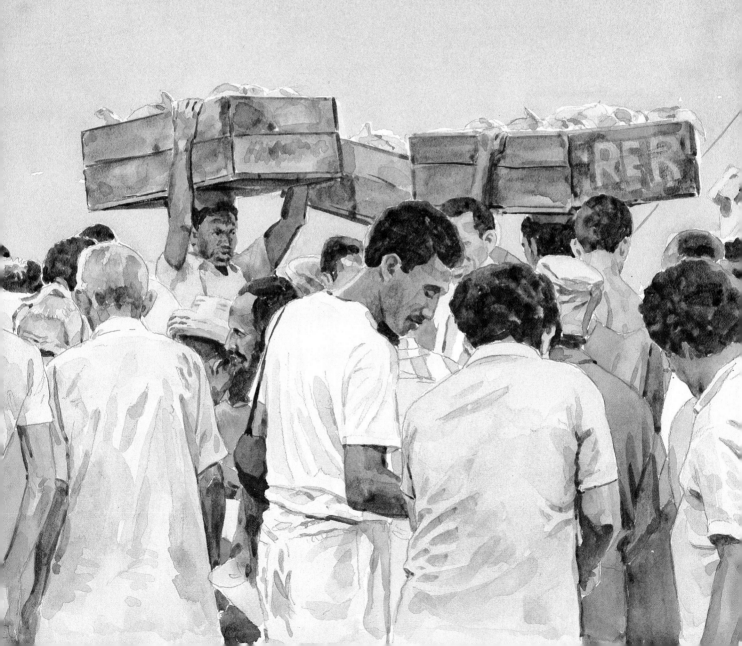

Outside they wandered through the covered stalls of the market. Paulo stared at the strange assortment of folk medicine. There were dried lizards, snake tails, porpoise jaws, and sloth claws, and vials of pure-white turtle fat. There were cures for backache, stomachache, headache, and fever.

There was a man selling crabs as blue as the sky. There were *açaí* in baskets with palm-leaf lids, gleaming pottery, and big bottles of yellow *tucupi*. The air was pungent with the smells of cooking.

The tide began to turn as black vultures soared in to feast on the discarded remains of fish on the mud flats. Paulo's father grew solemn. "I hope the river and forest will continue to give their gifts for all your birthdays. But there is so much ignorance in the world. The forest is burned for farming and ranching. In a few years the land is no good for anything. The earth is torn open for gold, destroying the streams and killing the fish. Our poor Amazon." Paulo saw how wet his father's eyes had become.

That night, as the steamer muscled its way upriver, Paulo
dreamed of dried lizards crawling over a blackened forest.

Early the next morning, Paulo went fishing. Before long he realized his canoe was being pulled upstream. His fishing line was as taut as a bowstring.

Hand over hand, he pulled in the line until he saw in the water a filhote bigger than his canoe. "We will be rich!" cried Paulo. "My father and I will take you to Belém and sell you at the market. It will take three big men to carry you on their heads!"

He looked down at the great, whiskered face in the water, and suddenly remembered his father's solemn words. He reached down and gently removed the hook. The fish slid back into the gloom.

"Good-bye and good luck, great fish," said Paulo.